Tidesong

Wendy Xu

Quill Tree Books
Imprints of HarperCollinsPublishers

Quill Tree Books and HarperAlley
are imprints of HarperCollins Publishers.

Tidesong

For information address HarperCollins Children's Books,
a division of HarperCollins Publishers,
195 Broadway, New York, NY 10007.
www.harpercollinschildrens.com

ISBN 978-0-06-295579-1 (paperback)
ISBN 978-0-06-295580-7 (hardcover)

The artist used an iPad with the Procreate art program to create the illustrations for this book.
Typography by Cat San Juan and Andrea Vandergrift
22 23 24 25 EP 10 9 8 7 6 5 4 3 2
❖
First Edition

To my students at HCMS and HCHS:
It's okay to stumble in life, figure it out,
and do things your own way.
This one is for all of you.

Once upon a time in a kingdom by the sea, a dragon fell in love with a human fisherman.
As her gift to him, she gave him the power to control the winds and tides, to become her near-equal in magic, and all their children afterward would inherit this gift.

But the dragon's clan was furious at her for leaving the sea, and to teach her a lesson, they sent a powerful hurricane that threatened to wipe away the kingdom.
The dragon, her fisherman, and their children combined their magic, and together, they pushed back the storm.

The dragon's clan knew they had met their match. They promised respect going forward.
As thousands of years passed, the dragon and fisherman's descendants lost their dragonlike features, but retained their powers over storm and sea: the Wu clan magic.
Wu water witches have the power to do the unimaginable with the ocean on their side.

Wu witches have turned a tsunami and raised ships from seafloor graves . . .
. . . spun wind into knots for sailors' safe passage . . .
. . . and, indeed, thrown the path of a hurricane.

To this day still, dragons, the rulers of all lesser sea spirits, come when a Wu witch calls to them.

Chapter 1

Lu, Mari, &
Sophie Wu
24 Greentree Rd

Whoa, can I touch it?
Don't! It's—
BZZ

HA
HA
HA
HA

Ugh, SOPHIE! You said you were gonna show us cool magic, not RUIN MY HAIR!

I'm sorry. I didn't mean to!
Aw, come on, Ellie, you gotta admit, it was funny . . .
WHATEVER! FREAK!

SOPHIE!

There you are!
Mama! Grandma!

Were you practicing spells for your little friends?
We passed them walking over.

Come home, girl.

We have BIG NEWS for you!

Sophie is of
course welcome to
stay and study
with us for a year
TA-DA!

Your big audition to the Royal Magic Academy!
Hmph. Though, knowing Auntie, this is a way for her to get help with CHORES for free. Still . . .
Sophie has such a GIFT, she MUST be admitted! What lucky parents to have such an incredibly talented daughter! This is the MOST POWERFUL RAIN SPELL EVER!

Two weeks later.
The train!
Make me proud, Sophie.
I'll try, Mama.

Oh, that
smells good . . .

I think I'm going to like it here!
GOOD CUP
BAKE

SHULAN HARBOR TOWN FERRY

Phew, found it!

Wow! What a view!

HEY!
THAT'S
MINE!

Stupid
SEAGULL, I
only got two
bites—

Huh?

Now docking!
Please make
sure you have
all of your
belongings!

You must be Sophie.

Y-you look like my grandma!

Morning, Auntie!

Yes, hello.

Potions
and
Charms

Rare &
Used Spells

Oh . . . wow. There is so much magic here!
Hmph. Yes. Magic.

But stop GAWKING like a seagull.

Tired already? We need to strengthen you up.

Mind the chickens, now.

EEEEEEEEEE

I have no food left to give.

Hi, Sophie! I'm Sage.
Nice to meet you, Auntie Sage.
I heard you graduated from the Academy with top marks.
Haha! Hilarious.
We can talk about that later. And just call me Sage.
Now, let's get you all settled in!
This will be your room.
Oh, wow!

It's beautiful!
Glad you think so! I'm going downstairs.
Yell if you need anything.

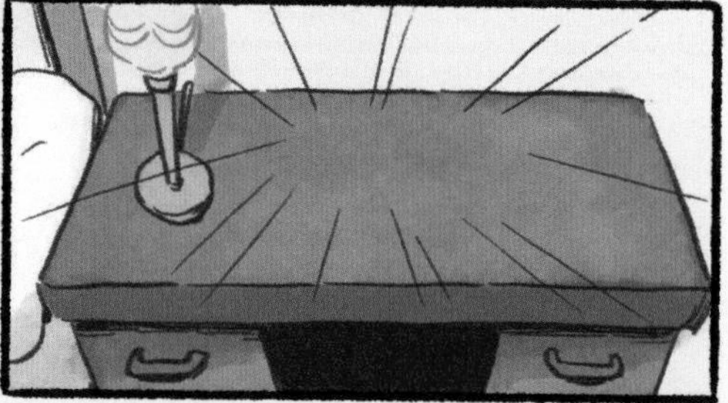

Sage . . .

Hrmph. She won't last three weeks on the island.

Doesn't seem to be raised right, no proper MANNERS, stares at EVERYTHING—
Auntie, I think you're being really unfair—
I cannot believe I agreed to this. Perhaps I thought she'd be cleverer.

Auntie! You've spent less than TWO HOURS with her . . .

. . . and besides, she's only TWELVE!

You might as well just show her some dog and pony tricks for that audition and send her along.

You're wrong, Auntie.

I'm going to become the MOST POWERFUL WITCH this family has ever seen.

Oh, shoot—

Knock, knock!
Almost forgot
a towel for
you. They're—

Oh my.
Are you
all right?

Well, okay!
I'll just leave this
here for you.

HWOOOOOOOO
SLAM

si
lence

YAWN

Z Z Z Z

Chapter 2

QUITE the wind last night. I could hardly sleep.

Sage has a few additional errands to run.

I will begin your training today.

Um . . . I don't know how to fly, yet.
Good heavens, child, who said ANYTHING about flight?

I want every stray feather off this porch within the hour.

Pull those weeds harder!
Knowing Auntie, this is just a way for her to get chores for FREE.

My chickens won't feed themselves!

Eat up. You need to be stronger.
She wants me to be stronger so I can work harder . . . ?
Ooh, that smells good! How was your morning?
SAGE! I did SO MANY CHORES! When do we begin training for real?!
This IS training, Sophie.
A very important part of it!

In our family, we master discipline and focus before even trying magic.

I dunno why I have to keep PEELING POTATOES and cleaning BEANS—
I've done a BILLION CHORES!
I ALREADY KNOW HOW TO FOCUS!
Look, Sage, let me SHOW YOU!
I KNOW how to do some magic—
SOPHIE, STOP!

I'm sorry, Sophie, but what you just tried indoors was foolish and dangerous!
Oh dear.

Here. Let's sit down.

Have some cocoa.

I'm sorry, Sage. I can't do anything right.

I get it. You have a big audition coming up. I was there once, too.

It's the most prestigious school in the whole kingdom!

If you want ANY kind of success as a witch, you HAVE to go!

EVERYONE knows that!

I didn't!
I guess things have changed since I went to school, though.
I feel like my audition was okay.
I don't remember that much, honestly!
. . . What?
Yeah, it wasn't that big a deal.
SHE'S MOCKING YOU. SHE THINKS IT'S DUMB TO GET THIS WORKED UP BECAUSE SHE HAD IT SO EASY. BECAUSE SHE'S SMART.
YOU HAVE TO PROVE YOURSELF, SOPHIE. AUNTIE AND SAGE WILL NOT TAKE YOU SERIOUSLY.

Whoa, hey, are you all right?

Y-yes! I just . . .

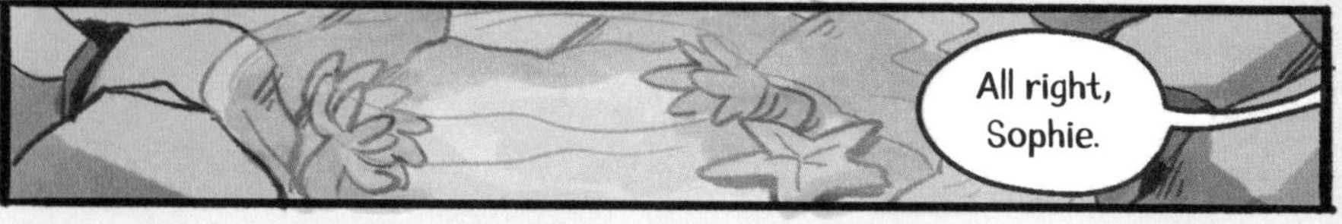

Since you already know some theory, let's hear it.
And you can take your boots off!
I'm gonna keep them on . . . anyway.
"All beings in this world have a well of aether, the foundation of all magic.
"Time and space are also interwoven with many, tiny aetheric knots.
"Depending on the method, both internal and external aether can be channeled."
Very good, Sophie. Watch closely—
This is our family's way.

That was AMAZING! I want to try, too!
Well, hold on—

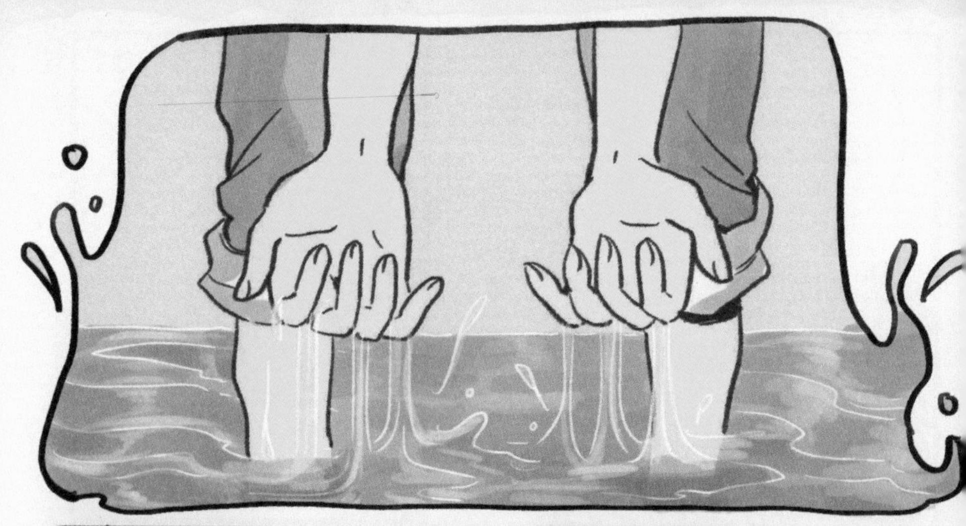

Hey, just because you know the theory, doesn't mean it'll work for you immediately.

WAIT!

Can I show you what I was trying to do before?
We're outside.
Well, okay, but—

Come on . . .

Sophie! You're going to be blown into the sea at this rate!
SLOW DOWN!

Sophie . . .
I screwed up again, didn't I?
I'm sure it was hard to hear over the wind, but I was trying to tell you that your stance was too stiff.
We can try again—
. . . Or, quitting the lesson for today is fine, too!

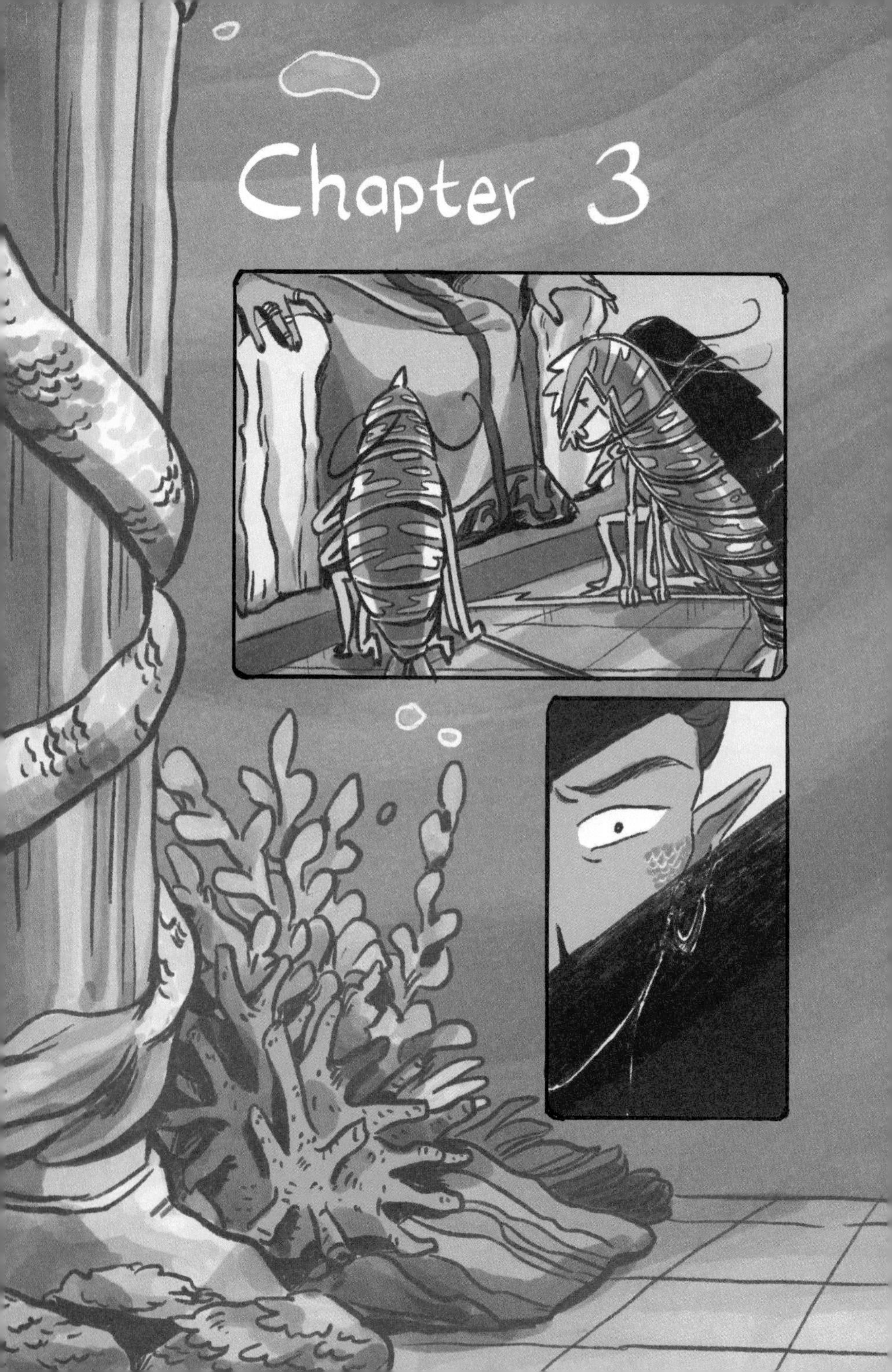
Chapter 3

rattle
rattle
Murmur
murmur

I thought you took care of this ridiculous wind LAST NIGHT, Sage. At this rate—
I'm going to the cove to talk to them, Auntie.
Good. I'M going to bed.

SLAM

SNORE

You don't have to sneak around, Sophie.

Oh, don't look so surprised.

I definitely knew you were following me.

But, hey.
I'm not as strict as Auntie.

Maybe watching me work will inspire you for our next lesson.
Not too far, now.

Here.

Hope you're ready.

Third Royal Clerk Jai Coralhorn of Water Dragon Bay at your service, esteemed Sage.
How may I serve today?
Oh gosh, Jai. Please just call me Sage.
Very well. And who is this? An onlooker?
I'm Sophie! I'm Sage's new apprentice!
Charmed.
Well met, Sophie.
So what business do you have with the Court of the Bay today?

AHEM

There's some kind of storm brewing in the Southern Sea.

The wind and currents have been off for days.
The merchants are starting to complain that their cargo ships are being held up at sea.
My spells are only effective for a certain radius . . . Is there anything you or the Court can do?
Or can I use a bigger spell?
I understand.
As you know, the Southern Sea is out of our jurisdiction, and they have not told us about any goings-on.

We could
ambassador,
would
discussion
Council, then
of Elders, not
the Baron
Trench
be passing
The Lady of
Coral does
dealing
Court and
the Scalies,
have to

We did not anticipate the involvement of other Undersea parties that would be affected by this use of magic, so please hold off a bit longer while we try to negotiate with them.

Can you just show me what kind of spell I can perform for now so I don't overstep whatever it is you're doing?

Here.

I want you to know that the First Council IS aware of the issue . . .

. . . but we cannot interfere with the weather-workings of the dragons in the South without their permission.

They are currently investigating a separate matter.

I will ask again on your behalf.

That's IT?!

You're NOT going to do any more magic?
I thought you guys would do a great big spell and FIX the problem!
Sophie, the entire ocean is a balanced and connected ecosystem.
The dragons know this best of all.
Part of Jai's job is to make sure that if we use magic in our part of the world, we don't upset the balance of the ocean in other parts.
That's why there's so much negotiation and communication with all the other dragons and their kingdoms.

We respect the dragons and work with them, directly and indirectly.

This is our family's responsibility as the longstanding link between this island and the sea spirits.

Okay, Sophie. Just like I showed you.
Tie the wind, nice and easy.
Relax your stance! Not so tight! It's a GENTLE breeze, not a gale!
Sophie! Don't fight it so hard!
Work WITH it!

That was a good try, Sophie, but you need to FLOW with the wind!
WHAT A FAILURE. AT THIS RATE, YOU WILL NEVER BECOME A REAL WITCH.
It's much easier with a light touch . . .
THEY'LL BE SENDING YOU HOME IN DISGRACE.
And just loop one strand over the other.
PARTY TRICKS WILL BE ALL YOU'RE GOOD FOR.
Look, I wrote the gestures down from when I first learned this!
Even I need a reminder sometimes!

. . .

SOPHIE! Feed the chickens, they're getting cranky!
Coming, Auntie!

PROPERTY of SAGE WU

Okay. I can do this.
I got this.
WHOA! I GOT THIS?!

"Knot the
wind
gently . . ."
IT
WORKED!
I really
did it!
Okay,
what's
next?
EEEK, cold!

I'm really doing this!
Splash
whoooooosh
Who knows how long it'll take the dragons to fix things!
I bet I could do it NOW and save everyone the trouble!

I'll show them all I'm worth more than some cheap spells! Auntie will be SO impressed—
SNAP

AAAAAA!

YOU FAILED, YOU FAILED,
YOU FAILED. . . .
. . . what?

SOPHIE!

You can EXPLAIN on the way home!

Are you cold?

I'm fine. How did you know where to find me?

The chickens are always watching, you know . . .

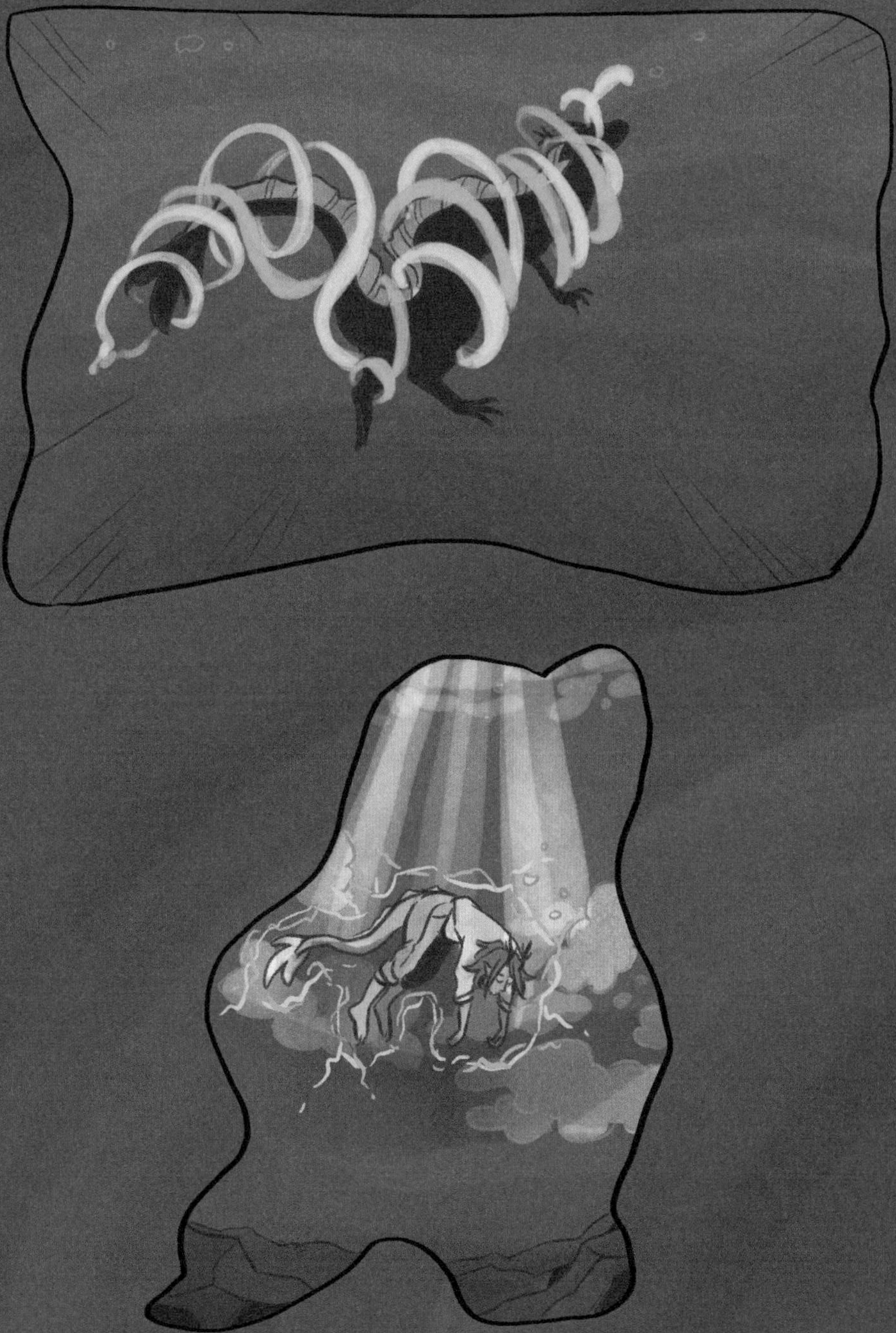

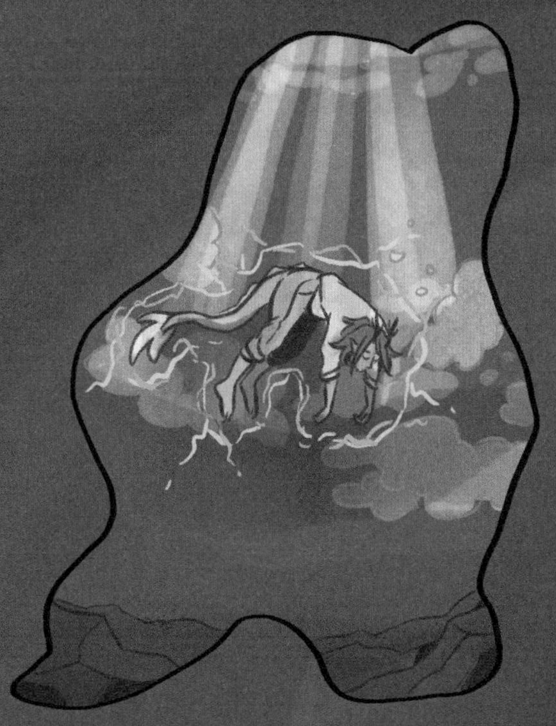

Chapter 4

Am I to hear that you STOLE Sage's spell book and snuck out like a common thief in the middle of the night . . .
. . . because somehow you thought you could fix a problem WE could not?

If all you want to do is show off, you should just go home.
Disgraceful!
You will be nothing but a failure at this rate—
Auntie, ENOUGH. She's been through a lot.
It's late. Let's all go to bed.

EAUGHHH!

CHILD!

Oh, thank goodness you're alive!

SOPHIE!

Go ahead, Lir.

I . . . I can't remember anything, except . . .

. . . my name, dark water, your face, and the feel of your magic.

Not all dragons can take on a human form.

Lir clearly comes from a powerful line. This is disasterous.

I'm back!

I've asked all over. None of the sea spirits know where he could be from.
Not even Jai or the rest of our dragons know.

Then we must let him stay here until he recovers or until we can contact his family.

Right. Lir, I'll show you to the guest room.

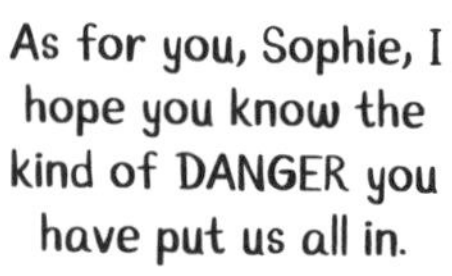

As for you, Sophie, I hope you know the kind of DANGER you have put us all in.

You have NO IDEA the kind of destruction an angry and powerful dragon can cause.
Floods. Entire towns swept into the sea.
But of course, an undisciplined, selfish CHILD would not care about the welfare of others, WOULD SHE?
We can only hope Lir's family are not the VENGEFUL type.

You are forbidden from doing magic until both Sage and I agree you may.
Now go to your room and think about what you have done.

Hello,
Sophie.

We did not get to speak much yesterday.
I apologize for my imposition.
What are you doing?

Reading.

May I join you?

I guess.
Do you KNOW what an angry dragon is capable of?

UHM, actually, I have . . . chores.

Seat's ALL YOURS! Best spot in the house!
Wait, I wanted to—

SOPHIE!!

We do not SLAM DOORS in this house!

Dinner
Thank you so much for this lovely meal!
What a helpful, well-mannered child.
Monday
Sophie, use more elbow grease! Heavens!
Lir has a way with animals!
Tuesday

Wednesday
Is something the matter?
No.
Thursday
Friday
He's just SO PERFECT and NICE and DOESN'T SLAM DOORS . . . Ugh.

Hello, Sophie.

What?
It's a lovely day!
Would you like to go to the beach?

Why, so you can show off by saving my life again?

No, I—

Sage!
Auntie . . .

Please, may I start my training again?
I REALLY have to practice for my audition.

Hrmph. Your punishment isn't over yet. Impatient as always—
Auntie, please let Sophie go back to her studies.

She's worked very hard in the last few days.

We'll start after lunch, right, Auntie?
Fine. Feed the chickens first.
Okay, Sophie. Let's try again.
Knot the wind.

Poor control,
bad stance.
You STILL
can't do
such a
simple spell?

I . . . we . . . did it.
Not bad, Sophie!
You got the second half down—
Hrmph. Lir did most of the spell.
Now, Auntie, that's really harsh—
I don't know how much of that magic was actually YOURS, Sophie.
Something's fishy here.
Sophie definitely did most of the spell.

Auntie—

You guys can go.
Sage, COME.

Hey. Let's go to the beach.

Your aunt was being so mean to you!
That's not fair at all!
I—

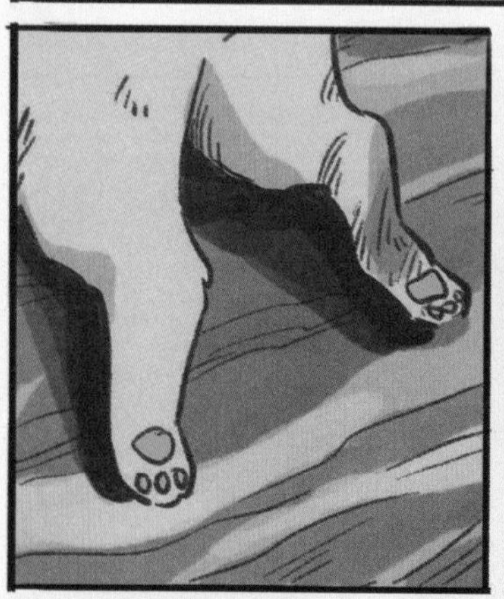

Oh, poor thing . . .

You're right, Lir.
My auntie IS mean to me.
I'm not good at anything.
Lir.
How can you help Lir if you can't even help yourself master one measly little spell for a silly school audition?
Maybe we can help each other.

I'll do my best
to help you find
your memories.
And since you
have dragon
magic . . .
. . . you can
help me study,
if you don't
mind?
Deal!

Chapter 5

He sure likes you, huh!
I guess so.
Followed me up from the beach, and he hasn't gone back.

Ugh.

I still don't get this theory.

Let me see, maybe I can—

Sophie! Lir! We're going on a little field trip.
Auntie had an idea.

Sophie, your magic's improved a lot, but this only seems to be when Lir helps you!
Auntie thinks you two are magically linked.
This lady we're going to see should be able to help us test this theory.

STILL NO GOOD ON YOUR OWN, SOPHIE. AT THIS RATE, YOU WILL NEVER BE.

CAFE

Ooh, SNACKS!

Three squid, please!

Is Auntie coming?
She's already there. Old friend of hers—this way!

Here we are! FINALLY!
Welcome, welcome. I'm Eugenia.
Come in and have some refreshments!
You must be tired after the walk!

Lanny, your family's here! Pour them some tea!

Eugenia's seen a lot of weird magic.
She's an expert in the field!
She's done research into things you wouldn't even think about!

She's weird, too. Hmph.
Lanny, you flatter me!

I have a hunch about what happened, but let me just take a look at you to make sure.

Now this is an unusual sight!
I've never before met a dragon with your kind of magic who couldn't shapeshift.

HUH?!
Let me put it this way, you two.
You know that magic runs through all of us like threads. Auntie told me about the incident.
From what I understand, that night, your magics became tangled when Lir saved Sophie's life.
This entanglement somehow locked Lir out of his dragon form entirely and erased his memories, as well.
It's not that unusual for young people's magic to go through some kind of strange turmoil at this age in your lives—after all, everything else is as well.
But I also suspect there is a strong underlying emotional resonance between you two that is making your magics knot.
Lir, what's the last thing you remember?

I told you.
Lir can't remember anything, Eugenia.
You might say that, Lanny, but I bet otherwise.
I'm going to get something. I'll be right back.
You kids just relax.
Our magics are TANGLED?
What if she can't untangle them?!
What if we're stuck together FOREVER?
Does this disqualify me from the audition?!
Now where did it go . . .
Would it matter, if it's something that can't be helped?!

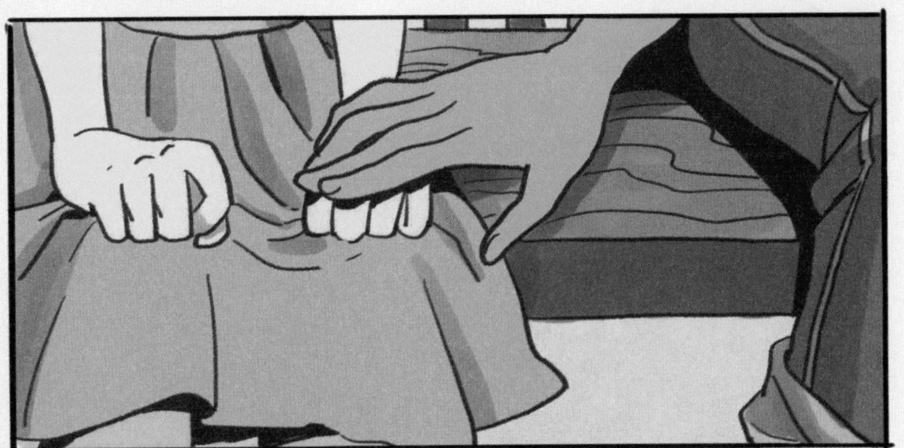

Lir . . . even though he's stuck here, he still wants to comfort me . . .

Ah, found it!

I misplaced my knitting basket. Here we are.

YARN?!

Ah, the little mouse speaks!

I'm glad Lanny here hasn't completely stolen your voice.
Now see here Eugenia, just because I believe in DISCIPLINE . . .

This is a seeking spell.
Whenever I've misplaced something, I visualize it coming to me on this silver yarn here.
I want both of you to place your hands on this piece of paper and make a circle with the yarn . . .
Very good.
Now, Lir, concentrate . . .

I . . . I did something terrible.
My father was furious.
I ran away . . . and then I got swept up in a current.
That's all I remember, for now.

The spell didn't work, did it.
Well, even though the memory we extracted was hazy, it's a starting point.
But I WILL say, you two are tangled up pretty tightly, like your magics WANT to be bound together!
You'll have to work together to figure out why, though.
Until you detangle yourselves, Lir won't be able to return to the sea.
It's a lot to take in, but I have faith you kids will figure it out.
Lanny, take the cocoa mix.
Stop standing on ceremony.
Um . . .
What is it, little mouse?

How did you know to try the string spell thing?
How did you know it might help bring back some of his memories?
Was it something you learned at the Academy?
Oh, I didn't go to the Academy.
I went to school right here on the island. We had great teachers!
And if you stick around on this earth for a while and keep an open and curious mind, you'll learn a thing or two, as well.

Sophie, mail for you from your mom and grandma.
And get changed! Those wet clothes will give you a cold!

"How's training coming, Sophie?" Fine, Mom. I just made a big, fat MESS and I can't fix it . . .
Magic used to be fun.
Even if it wasn't for anything.
Even if I was just making sparkles and clouds or whatever.
The one time I try to actually DO something with it, I end up LOCKING A DRAGON OUT OF HIS HOME.

Oh, Lir!
I brought . . . what is it called, cocoa.
With marshmallows.
I've never had this before.
Whaaat! It's my favorite!
Wow!
It's like MAGIC!

Hey,
Lir . . .

Aren't you just . . . a little afraid we won't be able to fix this?

I mean, you're great at magic and everything else, but I'm just a big failure . . . You saw how I can't even do a spell without your help.

Give yourself some more credit, Sophie.

Besides, there's no point in panicking, right?
I have faith that we'll figure something out.
It will be okay.
HE CAN'T POSSIBLY MEAN THAT.

MAYBE HE'S RESIGNED HIMSELF BECAUSE HE KNOWS, DEEP DOWN, THAT YOU'RE NO GOOD.

PROVE TO HIM YOU CAN FIND A SPELL.
PROVE THAT YOU CAN FIX THIS MESS YOU MADE. PROVE THAT YOU CAN WORK SOME IMPRESSIVE MAGIC.

NOBODY IS THIS KIND. NOBODY IS THIS GOOD. YOU'D BE AN IDIOT TO BELIEVE WHAT HE SAYS.

Ha, you're right. There's no point in panicking.
But we should get started right away, yes?

Oh, I guess—
Perfect! The sooner we figure this out, the sooner you can get your memories and everything else back and go home!

A textbook on intermediate magic?

Wow, a very . . . academic way to start.

As good a place as any, right?!

Chapter 6

Sophie . . . CHORES FIRST.

Y-yes Auntie!

Scary . . . She came out of nowhere . . .

Attempt 1:
Truth Potion

Attempt 2:
The Memory Map
Here, I just trace your hands and—
Whoa, it's working!
Oh, come on! This was JUST yesterday!
Well, it technically worked! I count this as a win!

Attempt 3:
Summon a Memory
from an Object

Lir, wait!
Come on!
Look, for ONCE things are going right for me!
Right. Okay.
I've NEVER been this good at magic before!
You wouldn't understand, you're just NATURALLY talented and—
SQUAWWWWK

Ew!
It's . . . so slimy.

Sophie! It's just a kappa!
Well, it's weird and gross and makes gross noises!

Hey there, little fella.

What're you gonna do, meditate in the tide pool?
It's worth a shot.
Well, that's DUMB.

Excuse me, but we've tried at least three spells from Sage's old textbook and NOTHING'S worked!
The SPELLS work! We just gotta try harder.

I'm not the one who has to TRY HARDER,
I'm the one who is STUCK HERE!

I've been going along with all your plans this whole time, Sophie.
But I don't think you care.
I think you just want me to be a conduit for your magic.

What—that's not—I—

It is, and you know it. You're just being selfish.

Lir, it's raining. We should . . . go . . .
You go.
I'm going to meditate in this DUMB TIDE POOL so I can try to get myself out of this mess, since you don't want to help.

My, is that young Sophie?
What are you doing here?
I CAN'T DO ANYTHING RIGHT!!!!

Ah, I see.
So you came here because you didn't want to go home and see Lanny—I mean, Auntie . . .

There you are. Cocoa.
Thank you.
Well, Sophie.
Tell me more about this angry little voice that says everything is your fault and that you're a failure.

I just . . . wanted to make everyone proud. Mama and Grandma, Sage. Especially Auntie.
I thought if I could learn the spells for the audition, I could help myself AND Lir.
And maybe Auntie would stop blaming me for all of this.
She acts like she HATES me and I dunno why!!

And Lir . . . he was right.
I thought I was trying to help.
But deep down I was only thinking of myself and getting into that stupid Academy.
Even after he was a good friend to me.
I'm awful.
Awful!
AND STUPID AND USELESS!
I'm sorry for coming, you barely know me and I just—
Oh, my dear—

You're not stupid and useless.

Auntie?!

Eugenia let me know you were here.
I came to bring you home.
But how?
Oh, we have our ways . . .

Ahem.

It would appear as though I owe you an apology, Sophie.
Judging by what you said, I was . . . very harsh on you.
Perhaps too much so.
Let me tell you a story, okay.
I was once a girl your age, Sophie.
This will take a while.
I'm going to start dinner.
Hush, Eugenia!
You will both stay, of course.
As I was saying . . . I grew up on this island with my parents . . .

. . . and my younger sister.
Lu was my best friend.
We were only two years apart.
She was beautiful, talented, fun-loving . . . more than a little spoiled.
Everyone thought she would grow up to head our family since I was the more serious and introverted one.
One day, when I was eighteen and Lu was sixteen, our grandmother called us to her side.
The time has come for me to choose my successor.

I have seen both of you girls grow up and my choice has been made.
Lan, you will continue the work of our family and become our envoy to the dragons after I am gone.
Grandmother, I thank you for this honor.
I will do my best to uphold our legacy.
WHAT?!
GRANDMOTHER, WHY NOT ME? I thought . . .
I have seen Lan practice her craft with a dedication unlike anyone else . . .
Sister . . .
But Grandmother—
. . . while you spent your time showing off to anyone who would watch you perform.
But when I was a child you said it would probably be me!
I, too, have worked hard!
Nonetheless, my choice has been made.

Lu, WAIT!
Leave her.
Her childish response shows me just how correct I was in my decision.
You have more important things to attend to, Lan.
That day, I realized my own sister could not even find it in her heart to be happy for me when Grandmother chose me instead.
Lu left soon thereafter. She never returned to the island.

Come on.

She wrote me a few weeks later, but she never apologized.
I was furious.
I promised that any child sent to me to learn our family's arts would be raised with DISCIPLINE . . . not indulged like my sister had been . . .
Lu still to this day will not apologize.
And neither will I.
But though you are her grandchild, you are not my sister.
I thought I saw too much of her in you, and I reacted very harshly without giving you a chance.
I'm sorry.
Auntie . . .

I'm a dragon.
I'm a dragon.
I belong to the sea.
Why can't I just TURN BACK?!

Lir.

Auntie, I—
Go.
We can finish this conversation later if you still need to talk.
She can sense his magic, even all the way up here?
She has great potential, indeed.
Hrmph. I suppose.
LIR!!!

I'M SO SORRY!
I WAS A HUGE JERK!
You were right . . . I was being selfish.
I promise I'll help you—REALLY help this time—figure out how to change back and go home!
We'll do this together, okay?

You're my friend and I care about you!

Thank you, Sophie.

I thought my connection to the sea was permanently broken . . .

But there's still some hope, I think.
I'll say so! You sure scared the fish . . .
Let's go home before we catch a cold.

THIS POWER THAT
SHAKES THE WAVES . . .
MY SON . . .

I HAVE FOUND YOU, AT LAST.

Chapter 7

I've never seen lightning like this before . . .
. . .

Jai, I was just about to contact you—this storm, it's—
We have an emergency on our hands.

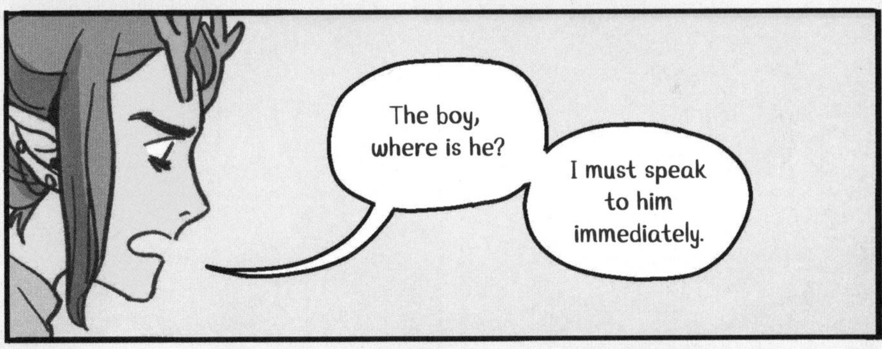

The boy, where is he?
I must speak to him immediately.

No flowery greetings?

It must be bad!

You. Boy. Come with me.

Stop it! You can't just grab people!

HEY!

Young lady, I am a dragon and I will not be spoken to in this way, nor will I be manhandled!
You did it first to Lir!

We're not going anywhere until you tell us what's going on and where you want to take him!

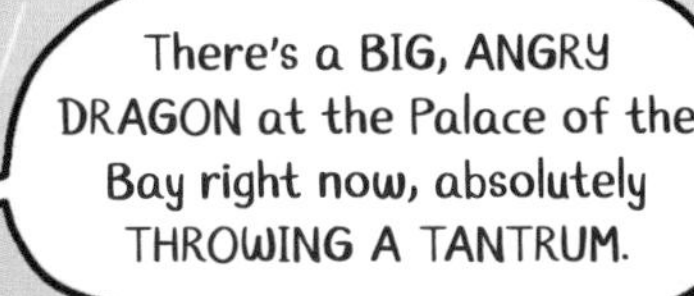
Tch. Kids.
Okay, listen. You see this rain?
There's a BIG, ANGRY DRAGON at the Palace of the Bay right now, absolutely THROWING A TANTRUM.

He is threatening to FRY US ALL TO OBLIVION unless we "hand over his son," and he is NOT PLAYING AROUND IF YOU LOOK OUTSIDE.
WHAT?!
When Sage told me she was hosting a strange, young dragon in her home—
Me?!
WHO ELSE WOULD IT BE?! Kids, I swear!
I had no idea you would be this much trouble for all of us!

Come to think of it, I didn't really pay that much attention, I had so much work . . .

REGARDLESS! You're both coming with me!

Auntie, this storm . . .
There's nothing we can do, Sage.

WHAT?!

We are in So. Much. Trouble.

Remember when I warned Sophie that we better hope Lir's family is not of the vengeful type?
Did Sage tell you about our situation?
She said there was some strange magic entanglement happening . . .

WHAT DO YOU MEAN, HE CAN'T CHANGE BACK?!

As it turns out, he is WANTED BACK HOME BY HIS VERY ANGRY FATHER!

There I was, ready to GO ON VACATION, LONG OVERDUE, I MIGHT ADD . . .

. . . when Lir's little TEMPER TANTRUM OF A BIG WAVE shook the seafloor and RUINED ALL OF MY WORK!
I stayed up all night reorganizing those papers . . .
AND THEN HIS FATHER SHOWS UP AND STARTS A HUGE, UGLY STORM! DO NEITHER OF YOU HAVE ANGER MANAGEMENT SKILLS?!
O-oh . . .

The sea gods help us all. I had no idea the island held a preteen runaway . . .

Can't you just tell Lir's father to . . . calm down?
Oh sure, let me just break all protocols of politeness to tell a DRAGON KING to CALM DOWN.

LIR!
Sophie, I'm scared. I can't . . .

I can't completely recall, but if it really is my father then I— I just—

Come on. We'll figure it out together.

I promise to protect you.

Sophie and Lir have to detangle their magics NOW.

We need more time to figure this out!
Well, maybe the BIG HONKING STORM and ANGRY DRAGON ROYALTY is an extra incentive here!

This . . . is all my fault again.

We should have figured this out sooner. I should have taken this more seriously.
I got so carried away with all these cool spells and finally having fun.
HOW COULD I HAVE BEEN SO STUPID?
AUUUGHHH!!

It's getting
really bad!
I'll say! We'd
better hurry!

We—we've been experimenting, but still we haven't figured out how to detangle yet.
That's nice, kid, but it's not helping.
Until Lir can transform back, there's literally nothing we can do to appease his father.
Is it the only way?
I swear, we've tried so hard—
You keep saying that, but the only thing that will fix this is DOING, not TRYING.
I'm so useless.
I don't even know where to start.

It seems so futile at this point.

My own selfishness brought this on. I deserve to be punished. I—

Wait.

Lir, I have never been more scared in my life, but I promised I'd protect you and I promised we'd do this together.

That night, when I got washed under the waves . . .

I didn't mean to, but I think I tangled my magic with yours to stay alive.
And then when you showed up and all my spells started working right for the first time, it was so amazing and powerful.
Sophie. Something's happening.
Keep going!
Whatever feelings you have to get out, talking is helping!
Oh, uh, okay! Um . . .
I really wanted to make everyone proud of me by getting into that stupid school and nailing the audition and—
Before you came, nothing was working . . . Lir?

Sophie! I remember now.
My father had entrusted me with a powerful weather working for the first time in my life.
The energy that spilled into the whole ocean because of me . . . I almost caused a hurricane.
My father managed to rein it in, but my magic affected the winds and currents all over the world.
The pitying looks people gave me.
I was an embarrassment to everyone. A weakling. A prince who didn't deserve to be one.

Lir! You are losing control of the magic!
How many MORE TIMES will you fail me?
It will take us MONTHS to sort this mess out.
You better prepare yourself to make amends to the court and the people of our realm.
I couldn't take it anymore.
So I ran away, like a coward.

When I saw you that night, in danger . . .
. . . I thought, at least I could do one thing right by helping you. Even if that didn't make up for my failure to my people and my father.

So it wasn't all my fault?
No! I let our magics tangle together to bury who I was.
I was so ashamed, I didn't want to remember anything.
But you're more than one mistake.
And you're more than one audition.
OH!

Oh, thank heavens. I might live to see my vacation yet.

Auntie!
They did it.

About time you fixed SOMETHING in your life, Prince Lir of the Southern Sea.

Oh no . . .
Your Esteemed Royal Majesty, King Ao Bing of the Southern Sea.

Chapter 8

My son!

Sophie! Are you all right?
Sage! Auntie!

You figured it out! Incredible! Well done!

Well done indeed, child.

Auntie . . . actually smiling . . . that's kinda scary.

Young Sophie. Everyone.

It is time for us to take our leave.
Thank you for your care of my son. I am glad to see him well and unharmed.

WHAT?!

I am a KING.

He is but a prince and barely a nestling.

AN APOLOGY?

How dare you, you impertinent little urchin?

EVERYONE needs to apologize when they've hurt other people!

Just because you're a grown-up and a king and Lir's dad doesn't mean you're perfect.
I saw it all, when Lir's memories came back to him! I saw it in our magics!
Lir looks up to you SO MUCH as his father and the leader of your realm! He always has!
He put on a brave face for my sake . . .
. . . but this whole time, he was so scared he wouldn't be able to face you, because you were so angry at him!

How could you be SO MEAN to him?
How could you ignore his feelings like this?

You . . . you impudent, defiant little . . .

You defiant little brat, Ao Bing!
How many times will you fail me, your king?
You are a prince but good for NOTHING!
Oh . . . I swore I'd never become like my father, and yet . . .

My son.
Forgive me, I am sorry for being so harsh with you.

Thank you, Father.

!
Thank YOU, Sophie.

Um!

So I guess this is good-bye?
Yes, but not forever.

As soon as I help my father put the Southern Sea back in order . . .

. . . and get a break in my princely responsibilities, I will return to see you.

Good-bye, Sophie, Sage, Auntie. Thank you for everything.

Can I GO NOW?!
This is a public relations disaster from here to the Southern Sea.
The PAPERWORK alone is going to take ages to sort out.
A king storming our palaces! Unheard of!
The Council of Elders will have many opinions on this, I'm sure.

I hope your BOYFRIEND was worth it— eh?

You. You're Lir's little friend, aren't you?

Oh? For me?

A note?
"Esteemed Clerk Jai, apologies if this approach is a bit untraditional . . .
but we, the Council of Elders, wanted to acknowledge and commend your hard work in assisting the King of the Southern Sea with the matter of His Highness, Prince Lir. They just stopped by the Palace of Pearly Fronds to praise your supreme skills and level-headedness. Thanks to you, the sea remains in balance.
"Please take several months off for yourself. Your coffers will be well stocked, and we will arrange for new clerks in your absence.
"You are hereby promoted to the rank of Third Lord of the Fan Corals. Congratulations.
Let us discuss this further upon your return to the Palace."

A-at last.
A vacation.
A PROMOTION!

I'm going to sleep for A THOUSAND YEARS.

SO LONG TO THE WORST BABYSITTING JOB EVER!!!!

Dear Sophie,
How are you?! Thank you for your last letter. Grandma and I were so happy to hear from you . . .
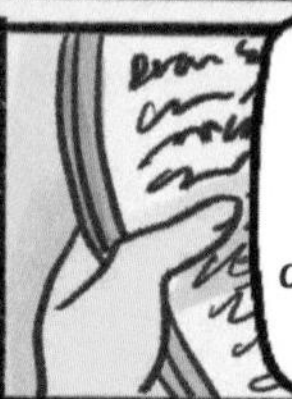
. . . and to hear that you're making progress. I can't believe you've been gone almost four months already! We miss you so much.

Now, as to the matter of audition spells . . .

So, Sophie . . .

How do you feel, now that you've had some time to recover?
Want to try your hand at magic again?
Well . . . I do want to continue training.
But I don't want to go to that school anymore.
I want . . . I want to stay here on the island and learn our family's traditions and magic.
For real this time.
I don't think I appreciated it when you showed me the first time.
But after working with Lir, and being his friend, and even after being scolded by Jai . . .
. . . I want to get to know their whole world better.
I'm not gonna learn that at the Royal Academy, right?
Hmm . . . We sure do have some arrangements to make!

Dear Mom and
Grandma . . .

What is the meaning of this letter, Sophie?
You DON'T want to go to the Academy anymore, girl?!

Well, I talked it over with Sage and Auntie and—

YOU WANT TO KEEP MY GRANDDAUGHTER AWAY FROM HER FUTURE, LAN? IS THAT WHAT YOU'RE TRYING TO DO?!

Lu, you old bat, will you CALM DOWN?

I want to learn more of our family's magic and work with the dragons!
Mistress Eugenia also said she'd teach me some of what she knows about strange spells—stuff that I can't learn anywhere else!
EUGENIA is in on this, too?!

Why of all the nosy—Sophie, be a good child.
You are far too young to know what you want out of life.
Listen to me and stop this foolish nonsense immediately.
Mother, maybe we should hear Auntie out—

Hello, Mari. Hello again, Lu.
I believe Sophie is making a well-informed decision, and we are happy to support her.

My, my. Such a fuss.
Is that little Lu I hear?

You've always had a chip on your shoulder, Lu.
Maybe you should work on that.
Don't PATRONIZE ME, LANNY!
You have basically KIDNAPPED and BRAINWASHED my grandchild!
Auntie, can I talk to Grandma?
Grandma, I'm not brainwashed.
And I promised Auntie, Sage, and Eugenia that I would work very hard.
So please don't worry.
You can always come visit, if you want to check on me.
Sophie, this obstinance will come back to haunt you, trust me.

What SACRIFICES?

Lu, you CHOSE to leave the island and you CHOSE to leave magic and OUR FAMILY behind!

Sophie, go back to the house.
Lu and I are LONG overdue for a talk.
Sophie, please think—
Grandma, Auntie.

I'll be waiting for you both.

It's soft, like dragon feathers . . .

Epilogue

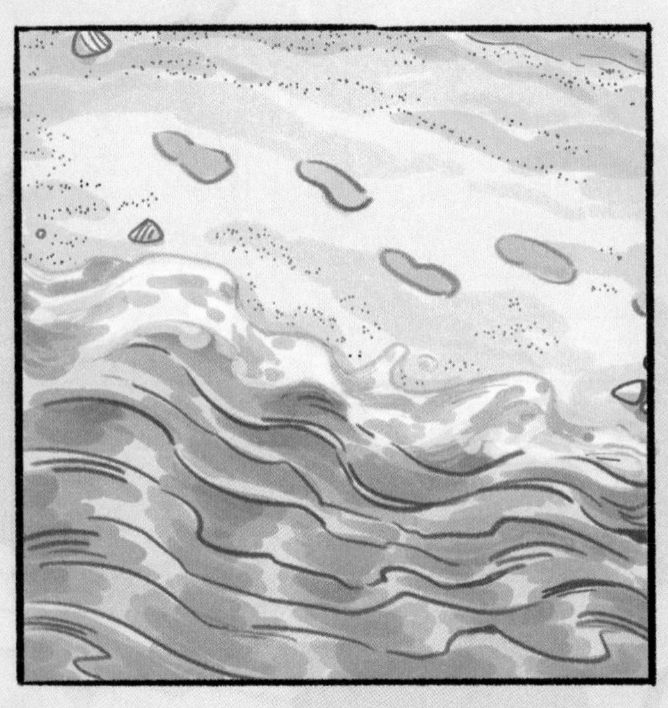

ACKNOWLEDGMENTS

Sometimes you don't know which memories you subconsciously tuck away in a drawer to pull out later for inspiration. When I was in college, my family went on a trip up the New England coast to Maine. In Acadia, I found beautiful water, lush green forests, and a charming seaside town (no water dragons to my knowledge), which, years later, would become fictional, magical Shulan. To that end, thank you to the wild New England forests and powerful Atlantic Ocean, and to my parents for bringing me there.

Thank you to Linda Camacho, my absolute superstar agent, without whom none of this would be possible. Thank you so, so much to Team *Tidesong*: Alex Cooper, who believed in the vision of this story from the beginning; Erin Fitzsimmons, for your wonderful cover treatment and art direction; Andrea Vandergrift, for putting this whole dang book together with the power of InDesign; and Cat San Juan, for turning my handwriting into an actual usable font! Thank you to Allison Weintraub for following up on all the important things I forget I also have to do as an author, such as submitting an author photo and social media stuff.

In no particular order, thank you to the friends who have encouraged me to become the best artist, and more importantly, the best person I can be: Shivana Sookdeo, Chris Kindred, Shannon Wright, Olivia Stephens, Hannah Vardit, Ethan Aldridge, Casey McQuiston, Steenz Stewart, Joamette Gil, Autumn Crossman, Kay O'Neill, Toril Orlesky, Jin Cha, Kody Keplinger, Sam Maggs, Adrienne Cho, Karuna Riazi, Aria Velasquez, Bianca Xunise, Erique Zhang, Cristy Yeung, Maya Pasini, Sabrina Chun, and Jade Feng Lee.

Thank you to my partner, Richard, for keeping the house together, the cat fed during all of my late nights, and providing endless love and support.

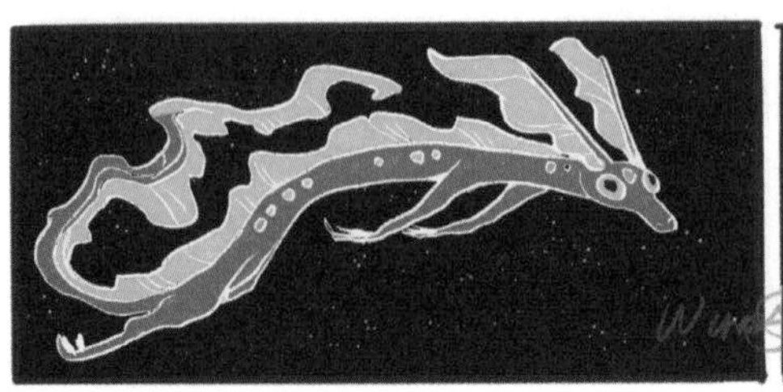

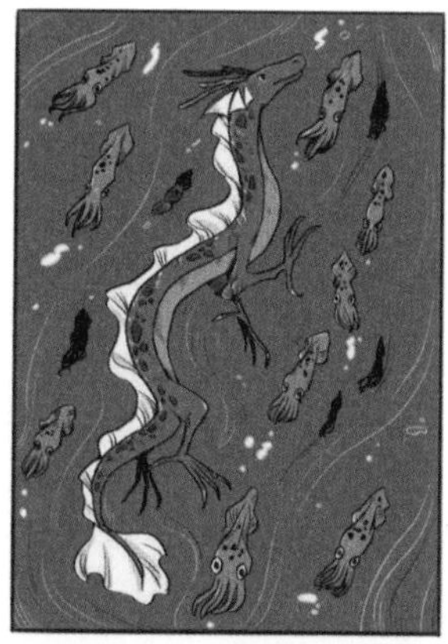

AUTHOR'S NOTE

A question a lot of people ask me is, "Where do you get your ideas from?" The dragons of Chinese mythology, which live under the sea and can shapeshift, provided a jumping-off point for the fantasy elements of this graphic novel. But I also spent a lot of time thinking about the different shapes of real-life animals and their movements to come up with the final designs for the water dragons and other creatures. Not just the bigger, charismatic ocean ones, like otters and sea lions (although I love those!), but the tiniest, almost invisible ones as well—plankton, the newborn fish, and all the little organisms that make up a coral reef. Not all of these designs made it into the final cut of the book, but they were all important when it came to building a fictional ecological backbone for the world of *Tidesong*. I am lucky to have grown up in New England, where we had all kinds of aquariums and coastal activities (tidepooling! crabbing!) for young people to learn about the incredible biodiversity of our oceans.

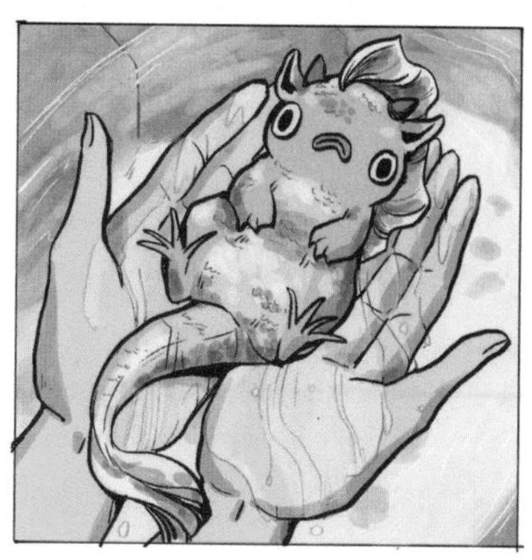

I encourage you all, if you can, to go to your school/town library or aquarium to find out more about local conservation efforts and what kinds of unique and wonderful creatures live in your area—you will be surprised, I promise.